Snow Much Mystery

by Marcia Thornton Jones
and
Debbie Dadey

illustrated by John Steven Gurney

A
LITTLE APPLE
PAPERBACK

SCHOLASTIC INC.

New York   Toronto   London   Auckland   Sydney
Mexico City   New Delhi   Hong Kong

To Lewanna Sexton — an expert at solving monster problems — MTJ

For Kristen Wathen — DD

ISBN 0-439-05873-2

Text copyright © 1999 by Marcia Thornton Jones and Debra S. Dadey.
Illustrations copyright © 1999 by Scholastic Inc.
All rights reserved. Published by Scholastic Inc.
SCHOLASTIC, LITTLE APPLE PAPERBACKS, and associated logos
are trademarks of Scholastic Inc.
THE BAILEY CITY MONSTERS in design is a registered
trademark of Scholastic Inc.

12 11 10 9 8 7 6 5 4 3 2 1   9/9 0 1 2 3 4/0

Printed in the U.S.A.   40

First Scholastic printing, December 1999

Contents

1
Blizzard

"Hip-hip-hooray!" Ben sang. "We have two whole weeks of vacation and we get presents besides. Mom said we could get our Christmas tree tomorrow." Ben, Annie, Jane, and their friend Kilmer were walking home from school.

Jane swung her empty backpack over her head. "The only thing we need to make it a perfect holiday is snow."

Ben shook his head. "No way. It's too warm."

Kilmer looked up at the bright sky. His broad forehead reflected the sunlight. Kilmer was in the fourth grade, just like Ben and Jane, but Kilmer wasn't an ordinary fourth-grader. Kilmer was at least a head taller than Ben, and his hair was cut flat across his head, almost like Frankenstein's monster.

"It will snow," Kilmer said with certainty. "Uncle Yetta is coming for a visit and there's always a blizzard when Uncle Yetta comes."

The moment Kilmer said his uncle's name a cold wind blew down Dedman Street. Trash cans rolled, and newspapers fluttered across yards. Annie pulled her coat collar around her neck and shivered as they got close to Kilmer's home, Hauntly Manor Inn. The inn looked more like a haunted house than a home. Shutters were broken and windows were cracked. Even the trees and grass in the yard were dead.

"Yip-pee!" Ben shouted. "It's snowing." Sure enough, a few fat flakes floated down.

Annie sighed. "It'll never snow enough to make a snowman."

But Annie was wrong. The next morning, snow was everywhere. Snow completely covered the cars on the street so they couldn't move. Everyone was snowed in.

The snow was so deep, Ben and Annie couldn't even get their Christmas tree, but that didn't seem to bother Ben one bit.

Ben was the first one outside. He rolled in the snow. He dived into the snow. He made huge snowballs and started a snow fort.

Annie and Jane joined him and they made a huge arsenal of snowballs. "I'm going to get Kilmer so we can have a real snowball fight," Ben said. "We'll blast you girls to the North Pole."

"You won't have time," Jane told him, "because you'll be digging your way home from Antarctica by the time we're through with you!"

The kids headed next door to Hauntly Manor Inn. Kilmer's cat, Sparky, almost ran them over as she dashed off the porch. "What got into that cat?" Jane asked.

"You'd think a monster was chasing her," Annie said with a laugh.

Ben kicked through a big snowdrift. "It would have to be a snow monster."

Jane suddenly grabbed Annie's arm. "Did you hear that noise?" Jane asked. "There's something weird in Kilmer's backyard."

"It was probably your stomach growling," Ben said.

Jane's dark eyes were big and round. "I'm serious. I think there may be a wild animal back there."

"Let's go see," Ben said, already trudging through the snow.

"No," Annie said, "it could be dangerous." But it was too late. Ben was already halfway around the inn. There was nothing for the girls to do but follow. When they reached the Hauntlys' backyard all three kids froze.

Ben blinked. Annie gasped. Jane gulped. None of them could believe their eyes.

2
Uncle Yetta

A snow sculpture stood dead center in the Hauntlys' backyard. But this was no ordinary snowman. It was so tall, the three kids had to bend their heads way back just to see its head.

"That is the biggest snowman I've ever seen," Jane said.

"It's not a snowman," Ben said. "It's a snow monster!"

His words hung frozen in the air as the back door to Hauntly Manor Inn flew open. Boris, Hilda, and Kilmer rushed down the steps. "Uncle Yetta came!" Kilmer shouted. "You're just in time to meet him."

Kilmer's mother, Hilda Hauntly, looked like she had been up all night. Her hair stood straight up in the air and the lab coat

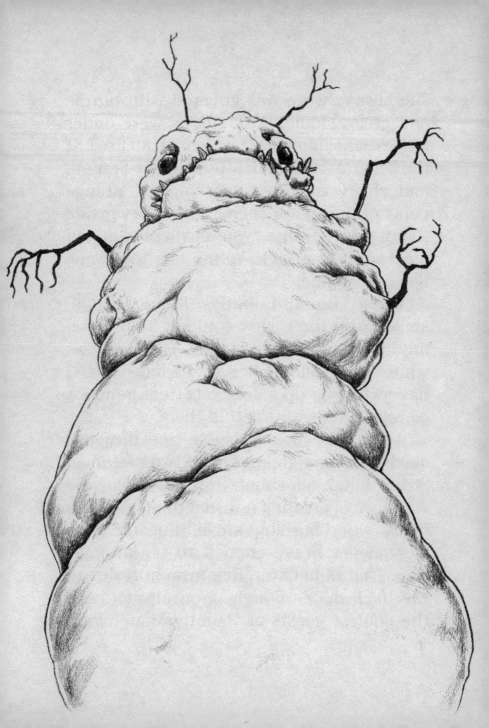

she always wore was covered with purple and green stains. Dark circles were under her eyes. Hilda was a scientist at F.A.T.S., the Federal Aeronautics Technology Station, and she was always working on strange concoctions in her secret laboratory inside Hauntly Manor Inn. "You must come in and meet our dear Uncle Yetta," she told Jane, Ben, and Annie.

When Boris Hauntly, Kilmer's dad, smiled, the three kids couldn't help noticing his two pointy eyeteeth. They were as white as the snow piled in the backyard. "I have whipped up a delicious treat in honor of Yetta's visit," Boris told them.

Annie gulped and Jane's face turned a sickly shade of green. The kids on Dedman Street knew all about Boris' cooking. He was always creating unusual treats on their black wood-burning stove, but the kids were never brave enough to try a single bite. That didn't stop Ben from hurrying to the back door, though. "You always have the coolest guests at Hauntly Manor Inn,"

Ben told Hilda, Boris, and Kilmer. "I can't wait to meet your uncle."

Jane looked at Annie and Annie shrugged. "Ben is right about one thing," Annie said. "The Hauntlys' guests usually stir up excitement."

Jane nodded as she followed Annie and Ben inside Hauntly Manor Inn. The kids were used to the dust and huge spiderwebs that covered everything. But they couldn't help noticing the icicles forming from the ceiling.

"Brrrrr," Annie said and zipped up her coat all the way to her chin. "It feels colder in here than it does outside."

Jane took the mittens out of her coat pocket and put them on. "It's so cold, ice is forming on the *inside* of the windows."

Sure enough, a thin layer of frost covered the cracked windows. Kilmer didn't seem to mind as he led the kids into the living room. "The air is a bit chilly," Kilmer said. "Uncle Yetta likes it cold because he lives up north where it never gets warm."

"I like it chilly as well," Boris said, pulling his cape tightly around him.

"Please," Hilda said, pointing to the bloodred sofa with giant claw feet, "make yourselves comfortable. Uncle Yetta will be here in a moment."

Ben, Annie, and Jane perched on the edge of the couch while Boris hurried to the kitchen. Annie made sure to keep her feet away from the claw feet. Once, she was sure she had seen them move.

Boris burst back through the swinging

door, carrying a tray of mugs filled with bubbling yellow liquid. "I prepared a traditional winter treat," he told the kids. "Won't you have some curdled milk topped with toasted sardine sprinkles?"

Jane gulped. Annie shook her head. Ben patted his stomach. "Boy, that looks great," Ben lied. "But we just had a huge breakfast. I don't think I could swallow another bite."

Annie nodded. Jane was ready to make an excuse of her own, but just then the front door blew open. A gust of Arctic wind swirled around their feet as the biggest, burliest stranger the kids had ever seen barreled into the living room. The floor shook with every step of his fur-covered boots.

"Uncle Yetta!" Kilmer yelled and ran across the room to give his uncle a big hug. Uncle Yetta laughed, but it wasn't a normal laugh. His laughter was more like a roar.

Uncle Yetta had curly white hair, a thick white beard, and white hair even on his

knuckles. He threw his arms around Hilda and then shook Boris' hand.

"These are my friends," Kilmer told his uncle. "Annie, Ben, and Jane."

Uncle Yetta grinned and shook their hands. Annie noticed that Uncle Yetta's skin was as cold as an ice cube and had a faint blue tinge. Jane was too busy staring at the floor around Uncle Yetta's boots to notice his skin. "Look," she whispered to Ben.

Ben glanced at the floor. Huge puddles of water were forming around Uncle Yetta's giant boots. The puddles were getting bigger and bigger as his ice-crusted fur coat started to drip. "It looks like Uncle Yetta is melting!" Ben whispered.

"Bailey City is a sight for sore eyes," Uncle Yetta was saying. "But I forgot how hot city living is."

"Forgive me," Hilda said as she hurried from the room. "We will turn down the heat so you will be more comfortable."

"If it gets any colder in here my blood will freeze into ice cubes," Jane hissed.

"Shhh," Annie whispered. "Don't let Boris hear that. He might like the idea of a blood-cicle."

"Besides," Ben said, "the Hauntlys would never make it so cold in here that we'd freeze."

But by the time Hilda got back in the room, the temperature had fallen so low, the three kids were shivering. "I think we'd better go," Annie said as politely as she could.

Jane and Ben nodded. "It was nice meeting you," Ben said as the three kids hurried out the kitchen door.

As soon as they stepped into the backyard, Annie gasped. "The snow monster has escaped!" she yelled.

3

Abominable Snowman

"What are you talking about?" Jane asked.

Annie pointed to the middle of the Hauntlys' backyard. "The snow monster," she said. "It's gone." Sure enough, the huge snow sculpture was missing. There was only a deep mound of snow where it had stood.

"Annie's brains must've frozen," Ben teased. "Snowmen can't just walk out of backyards."

"Ben's right," Jane added. "The snowman probably got knocked down. After all, there *is* a big pile of snow where the snow sculpture was."

Ben nodded, pointing to the shining sun. "Either that or it melted."

Annie looked at the sky. "I guess you're right," she finally said.

"In fact," Jane said with a grin, "I bet so much snow has melted that cars can get down Dedman Street now. That means you can get your Christmas tree."

"Let's go," Ben said with a whoop and rushed toward his own house. Jane hurried after him.

Annie glanced once more at the empty spot in the middle of the yard before following her brother and best friend around Hauntly Manor Inn. She hadn't gone far when she froze in her tracks.

"What is it?" Jane asked as she and Ben kicked their way back through the snow. Annie pointed at the ground. Jane and Ben saw huge footprints leading right to the Hauntlys' front door.

"Those look like a snow monster's footprints to me," Annie said with a gulp.

Ben laughed so hard he sat down in the snow. "Exactly how many monster footprints have you seen lately?" he asked.

Jane patted Annie on the shoulder. "Ben is right. These footprints probably belong to Boris."

"Then why didn't we see them before?" Annie asked. She didn't wait for her brother or friend to answer. "I know why," she told them. "Because those prints belong to a snow monster!"

"Don't be silly," Jane told Annie. "There are no such things as snow monsters."

"Wait," Ben interrupted. "That's not exactly true. There have been sightings of lots of snow monsters, like the Abominable Snowman."

"There is no such thing as a snow monster," Jane said again. "Besides, the tracks lead right up the front steps and through the door of Hauntly Manor Inn. We were just there and there wasn't a single giant snowman hidden anywhere."

"AAAAAHHHHHHH!" Annie screamed and fell down in the snow. She was shaking.

"Are you really that cold?" Ben asked.

"I'm not shivering from the snow and ice. I just realized that Jane is wrong," Annie said with a trembling voice. "The Abominable Snowman is inside Hauntly Manor Inn, and his name is Uncle Yetta!"

4
Melting

CREAK!

"Somebody's coming," Annie squealed. Ben, Annie, and Jane scrambled into the bushes just as the front door of Hauntly Manor Inn swung open.

BOOM. BOOM.

Uncle Yetta stomped out onto the porch. He was so tall, his head brushed the top of the porch. "Argh!" Uncle Yetta roared. "The snow is melting!"

Hilda, Boris, and Kilmer rushed outside. Boris stayed in the shadows, but Hilda peered up at the sky. "Don't worry," Hilda said, patting Uncle Yetta on the back. "Everything will be fine. I have a plan."

The Hauntlys and Uncle Yetta disappeared inside the house. Jane stared at the puddle Uncle Yetta had left in front of the

door. "I wonder what kind of plan Hilda has in mind."

"Maybe she's planning on making snow cones," Ben suggested. "After all, Boris is a terrible cook."

"He's not terrible if you enjoy weird stuff like curdled milk and sardine sprinkles," Jane said. "Some people might like that kind of food."

"Not me," Ben said. "Give me pizza any day."

"Don't you both get it?" Annie asked.

"Get what?" Jane and Ben asked together.

Annie scrambled out of the bushes and brushed the snow off her knees. "I don't know what Hilda's planning, but whatever it is, it's bound to be trouble."

Ben stood up and puffed his chest out. "That's okay, I can handle trouble."

"That's because trouble is your middle name," Jane said with a giggle.

"I'm not kidding," Annie said. "I have a

feeling that things on Dedman Street are about to get worse, a lot worse."

Just then a huge gust of wind blew and snow started falling. Ben stared up at the sky. Snowflakes the size of Ping-Pong balls floated onto his face. "What happened to the sun?" he asked.

"I don't know," Jane said, "but I guess you won't get your Christmas tree today after all."

"I think I know what happened to the sun," Annie said.

Ben tried to catch a snowflake on his tongue. "What are you? The weathergirl from station WMTJ?" he asked.

"No," Annie explained. "I'm the very worried neighbor of the Abominable Snowman."

5
Closed

"Closed?" Annie said after listening to the radio the next morning. "How can the mayor close the whole city?"

Ben shrugged. "The mayor just did it, so what difference does it make?" Ben looked out the window of their family room. Snow had drifted halfway up the window and more snow was falling.

Annie shivered. "I wanted it to snow for Christmas," she said, "but this is getting ridiculous. I've never seen this much snow in my life."

"An Eskimo hasn't seen this much snow," Ben added.

"I'm supposed to meet Jane in front of Hauntly Manor Inn," Annie told him. "Do you want to come with me?"

"Sure," Ben said. "I want to try sledding

in this stuff." Ben and Annie grabbed their hats, boots, gloves, snow pants, coats, and scarves. They were so bundled up, they looked more like clumps of clothes than people.

"If I fall down," Annie complained to her brother, "I'll never be able to get back up."

Ben laughed. "Don't worry, I'll bring food out to you every couple of days or so."

"Very funny," Annie said, sticking her tongue out at Ben.

Jane was just as bundled up when they met her in front of the inn. "Isn't this the craziest weather you've ever seen?" she asked through her scarf.

"And I know what's causing it," Annie said.

Ben slapped a gloved hand to his forehead. "Oh, no," he said. "You aren't going to start talking about snow monsters again, are you?"

Annie stomped her foot. "I think the Hauntlys are somehow making this snow."

HAUNTLY
MANOR
INN

"Why would the Hauntlys want to do that?" Jane asked.

"They want to make Uncle Yetta happy," Annie explained. "He said he loved the cold and snow. And didn't Kilmer say it always snows when Uncle Yetta visits? I bet the Hauntlys make sure it snows."

"You're nuts," Jane said, knocking a snowflake off the tip of her nose. "Nobody can make it snow."

"Maybe someone can make snow," Ben said.

"What are you talking about?" Annie asked.

Ben gulped and hopped up from the snow. "I didn't want to tell you this, but last night I saw Hilda working in her laboratory from my bedroom window."

"What does that have to do with anything?" Jane asked.

"She was making snow," Ben said matter-of-factly.

Jane laughed and rolled her eyes. "Right, and tomorrow I'm going to make a tornado."

Annie ignored Jane and threw a snow-ball at Ben. "Why didn't you tell us sooner?"

Ben shrugged. "I didn't want you to get all crazy and start blaming stuff on Hilda. After all, she only made a few flakes. She couldn't have made a whole blizzard."

"Nobody could do that," Jane agreed. "I can make a few ice cubes in our freezer, but I can't coat the town with icicles."

"Right now I'm not worried about snowflakes. I'm scared of what's digging through the Hauntlys' yard," Annie told her friends and pointed at a big lump in the snow. It was moving. And it was coming right for her.

6

Monster Invasion

Something was burrowing under the snow.

"A snow monster is digging its way out of the back of Hauntly Manor Inn and coming straight toward us," Annie whimpered. "We're doomed!"

"We're doomed, all right," Ben said. "But not because of a snow monster. We're doomed to listen to your snowman fairy tales."

"We don't have time to argue," Annie told her brother. "We have to get out of here. Fast!"

Annie didn't wait to hear another word. She turned and tried to run, but she didn't get far. Her boots sank into the deep snow. The more she struggled, the more stuck she became. "Get me out of here!" she screamed.

Jane and Ben hurried to Annie. "Stop wiggling," Jane said. "You're just making it worse."

"You have to help me," Annie gasped. "Before it gets me."

The three kids looked across the Hauntlys' yard. Whatever was digging its way through the snow was halfway to them.

"I'll help," Ben said. Annie reached her hand out to Ben, but he didn't take it.

"I'll help," he said again, "by proving there is no snow monster." Ben took a giant step toward the moving mound of snow.

"We have to stop him," Annie told Jane, "before that monster reaches up through the snow and drags Ben down!"

Jane grabbed Annie's arm and pulled her out of the huge snowdrift. "I'm not so sure that's a snow monster," Jane told Annie. "But there's one way to find out!"

Annie groaned when Jane trudged

through the snow after Ben. Annie thought about running back to her house and hiding in a closet. But she would have a hard time explaining to her parents that her brother and her best friend had been dragged off by a giant snow monster. There was only one thing left for Annie to do. She had to go after Ben and Jane.

Ben and Jane quietly made their way toward the moving mound of snow. They reminded Annie of two cats creeping up on a mouse. Annie fell in behind them. The three kids stalked the moving mound of snow until they were so close Annie could hear the crunching of snow from beneath the burrow.

Suddenly Ben pounced and clawed through the snow.

"Yeow!" he screamed and stood up. He held Sparky by the tail, and Kilmer's cat did not look happy.

Sparky hissed. She growled. Then she hissed some more. Ben dropped Sparky and jumped back. Kilmer's cat wasn't like

most cats. Instead of running, Sparky turned to pounce on Ben.

"RUN!" Ben screamed as he dodged the angry cat. He tore around Hauntly Manor and headed straight for the backyard. Sparky was close at his heels. Annie and Jane raced after them but it was hard to move since the snow was so high and they were bundled up in coats and scarves and boots.

Ben screamed again.

"Oh, no," Jane said. "I think Sparky just caught up with Ben."

Annie and Jane rushed around the inn and skidded to a stop. Annie gasped and Jane gulped at what they saw in the Hauntlys' backyard.

Ben had collided with Uncle Yetta and was sprawled on the ground, buried in deep snow. Uncle Yetta reached down and, with one arm, lifted Ben high up in the air before gently placing him on the frozen ground. But that didn't scare Annie and

Jane as much as the snow sculptures that filled the Hauntlys' backyard.

Frozen monsters made of snow were lined up everywhere.

"It's a monster invasion!" Annie whispered.

7
Winter Monsterland

There was a two-headed snowman, a snowman with one giant eye, and a snow-man with arms that looked like tentacles.

"I'm getting out of here," Annie said. But before she could run, Kilmer, Boris, and Hilda flung open the back door and stepped out onto the rickety porch.

"Isn't this snow wonderful?" Boris asked. Boris wore his cape pulled up to his cheeks. He had on sunglasses and a big hat that cast his face in deep shadows so that not a ray of winter sun could touch his skin.

"It's a winter wonderland," Hilda added. She was bundled up in a black coat and pointy black boots.

"It's a winter monsterland," Annie whispered under her breath.

"Shhh," Jane warned as Kilmer kicked

his way toward them. "Don't let the Hauntlys hear you. You might hurt their feelings."

The Hauntlys hadn't heard. They were too busy talking to Uncle Yetta.

"A party!" Hilda suddenly exclaimed and clapped her hands. "That sounds wonderful."

"Party?" Jane asked.

Kilmer nodded. "Uncle Yetta was just about to treat us to a snowland party," he explained.

"I like parties," Ben said. "Especially when they serve cake and ice cream."

"It looks like the entire neighborhood is filled with nine feet of ice cream," Jane said with a laugh.

Annie didn't even smile. She tugged on Jane's coat and leaned close to whisper. "I don't think this is a snowland party," she said. "I think it's a monster party and all these snow sculptures are Uncle Yetta's snow monster friends."

"Don't be silly," Jane told her. "They're

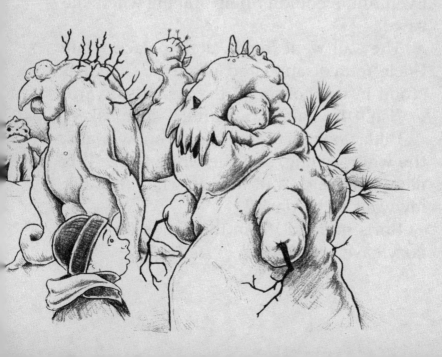

only snowmen. A party sounds like fun." Then she hurried to join the others.

Annie sighed before following Jane and Ben. She didn't have too much time to worry because Uncle Yetta kept them busy.

"Every winter wonderland needs a snow palace," Uncle Yetta explained. Then he showed everybody how to carve out frozen bricks from snow. He carefully lined them up until they had a house built entirely of snow. The snow sparkled in the sun as if it were made from billions of tiny diamonds. Even Annie couldn't help smiling when she saw it.

They all went inside their palace while Uncle Yetta disappeared inside the shed that stood in the corner of the Hauntlys' yard.

"Isn't the palace beautiful?" Jane asked.

Hilda looked at the white snow walls, the white ceiling, and the white floor. "It is nice," she said, "but it is so white. I prefer my walls to be dark."

Boris nodded. "Like the inside of a nice cozy cave," he added.

"Enough playing house," Uncle Yetta boomed from outside the palace. "I'm ready to glide!"

They all rushed outside to find Uncle Yetta pulling a huge board he'd turned into a sled. "Climb on," Uncle Yetta said with a grin. "We're going for a winter ride."

Hilda laughed. "What fun," she said as she glanced at the blue sky and bright sun. "But I am much too tired to join you. After all, I was up all night working, and I believe I will need to do a bit more work tonight."

"I don't think everyone can go anyway," Ben said. "No one is strong enough to pull a sled piled with people."

But Ben was wrong. Once Boris, Kilmer, Ben, Jane, and Annie were comfortable on the sled, Uncle Yetta picked up the rope and tugged. The sled glided easily over the snow. Uncle Yetta pulled them down Dedman Street and all the way to Bailey City Park. Cars were stuck in the massive snowdrifts, but Uncle Yetta didn't have any problems

making his way through. Soon the sun began to shine brightly and the temperature climbed so high that they needed to unzip their coats. Icicles dripped and the snow started to melt.

Uncle Yetta was sweating so much he looked like he was melting, too. "We better get back to the Hauntlys' house," Annie said, "before Uncle Yetta turns into a giant mound of slush."

Ben rolled his eyes. "Are you still stuck on that crazy idea?" he asked.

Jane shrugged. "It does look like Uncle Yetta is melting," she pointed out.

"He's just sweating because pulling a sled full of people is hard work," Ben told them.

Uncle Yetta slowed down. He glanced up at the bright sun and mopped off his forehead. "We must get back," he said over his shoulder. He was no longer smiling.

Then he jerked on the rope and they sped off toward Hauntly Manor. Uncle Yetta moved so fast it felt like they were bobsledding in the Winter Olympics. He didn't stop until they reached the backyard of the inn.

"I will go and speak with Hilda," Boris told Uncle Yetta. "Do not worry."

"I think we all need to worry," Annie said as Kilmer and Uncle Yetta followed Boris into Hauntly Manor Inn.

8

Canceled

Annie pointed to the snow sculptures. "The snow monsters have moved again!"

"You're just imagining things," Ben snapped at his little sister. "Those snow creatures are in exactly the same positions they were before."

Annie shook her head. "I know they've moved and I know we're in big trouble. Snow monster trouble. Uncle Yetta is the Abominable Snowman and he's bringing his Arctic monster friends to Dedman Street."

"What would an Abominable Snowman want in Bailey City?" Jane asked.

Annie shrugged. "It's a nice place for a vacation."

Ben laughed. "I think you need to ask

Santa to bring you a new brain for Christmas. Your old one is worn out."

"That's just it," Annie complained. "There won't be anything for Christmas. Santa is smart enough to stay away from a street filled with snow monsters."

"You're nuts," Jane said, patting Annie on the shoulder. "Even if there were an Abominable Snowman on our street —"

"Six of them," Annie interrupted, pointing at the sculptures.

"Even if there were a *million* of them," Jane said, "Santa wouldn't be afraid of them."

Ben grinned. "Cool. We could have a fight between Santa and the snow monsters. We could sell tickets."

"No." Annie stamped her foot. "Don't you get it? Santa won't even be able to get to our street if Hilda has her way. She's going to keep on making snow, snow, and more snow."

"What's wrong with that?" Ben asked.

"It's our vacation and I love to play in the snow."

Annie tramped through the Hauntlys' yard and kicked a huge pile of snow. "The problem is that if it keeps snowing like this, nobody will be able to do their Christmas shopping and that means no candy, no trees, and *no* presents."

Ben gasped and for the first time really looked worried. "No presents?"

"Don't get upset," Jane told Ben. "Uncle Yetta is not a snow monster — he's just a big guy who likes to play in the snow."

"I hope you're right," Annie said. "Because if the townspeople even suspect that the Hauntlys are the reason Christmas has to be canceled, they'll run them out of Bailey City before we can say Jack Frost."

"They can't do that," Ben said as he stomped across the Hauntlys' backyard. "The Hauntlys are our friends."

"You're getting upset over nothing," Jane insisted. "Even if Hilda is a mad scientist, there's no way she can make that much snow."

Ben pounded his fist into a snowdrift before looking at Jane. "But what if Annie is right?" he asked. "Do we want to take that chance?

9
Monster Blizzard

"It's a blizzard," Ben shouted the next morning as he and Annie stepped outside to meet Jane.

Annie held up her hand to block the rapidly falling snow. "The snow is falling so fast."

"And it's getting worse," Jane pointed out. "My mom hasn't been able to get our car out of the driveway for three days in a row. At this rate, she won't be able to go shopping until June."

"Whoever heard of Christmas in June?" Annie asked.

"I like snow," Ben said, brushing huge clumps of snow off his shoulders, "but this is ridiculous. I think I'm turning into a snow monster myself."

"You are a monster," Annie said with a

giggle. "But Jane's mom isn't the only one stuck at home. All of Bailey City is closed down, even the mayor's office."

Ben grabbed a sled from the porch and threw it on the ground. "I sure was looking forward to getting our Christmas tree," he complained. "I guess that will have to wait."

"We'll be lucky if we get to buy a candy cane at the rate this snow is falling," Jane said. "It looks like Christmas is history."

"Presents aren't the most important part of Christmas," Annie reminded them.

Ben sat down on his sled. "But it's my favorite part," he said.

"Right now we have to think about the Hauntlys. If the mayor or anyone else figures out that Hilda is behind all this snow, the Hauntlys will be in big trouble," Jane said.

Ben shrugged. "I guess we should do something."

"But what?" Annie said.

"Let's go sledding and maybe we'll think of a way," Jane suggested. They stopped at

Hauntly Manor Inn to pick up Kilmer. Kilmer had a black sled with bat wings on the side. They all headed to Piper's Hill.

Just about every kid in Bailey City was sledding at Piper's Hill. Ben almost collided with a third-grader named Eddie. Annie shared her sled with a girl named Liza. Jane raced Melody down the hill and barely beat her. Kilmer's sled was so fast Ben went down the hill with him several times. "This is the best sled ever," Ben told Kilmer.

"Uncle Yetta gave it to me," Kilmer told

Ben. "Speaking of Uncle Yetta, I think I'll go see how he's doing." Kilmer waved and walked away carrying his bat sled.

Finally Jane's face was so cold she felt numb. "Let's go home and get some hot chocolate," she suggested.

"That's a perfect idea!" Annie said with a grin.

Ben nodded. "Sounds good. It's too bad we didn't think of a way to help the Hauntlys."

Annie smiled. "Don't worry," she said. "I have a plan."

10

Annie's Plan

Annie pulled Jane and Ben close. Snow continued to fall as Annie whispered her plan.

"It will never work," Jane said, shaking her head.

"But we have to try," Annie argued. The snow had been falling so fast a layer was piled on her shoulders. She brushed it off before continuing. "If we don't do something, Christmas will be canceled and we'll be trapped inside our houses forever. And that means no presents, no trees, not even a single sugar cookie."

Ben gasped. "I'm ready to try Annie's plan," he said. "I don't want to miss Christmas presents from anyone."

"Great! But let's forget about packages

and bows for now," Annie told her brother. "We have to think about the Hauntlys."

"Well," Jane said slowly, "I guess it won't hurt to try. After all, the Hauntlys are our friends. We have to help them if we can."

Annie patted Jane on the back. "That's the spirit," she said.

Ben nodded. "I guess there's no time like now to put your plan into action."

"That's right," Annie said. "We'll hurry home and get everything we need. Meet in front of Hauntly Manor Inn in exactly thirty minutes!"

The snow had stopped falling by the time they met on the sidewalk in front of the Hauntlys' house. Annie carried a big basket. Ben had a paper bag. Jane's backpack was stuffed. "Do you really think this will work?" Jane asked.

Annie nodded. "If it doesn't, then we'll know Uncle Yetta is just a snow-loving uncle."

"Then let's do it," Ben said and led the

way through the deep snow to the Hauntlys' front door. They passed three new snow sculptures on the way.

"Those weren't there before," Annie whispered. She didn't like the fangs one snow sculpture had or the four arms and ten horns on the one next to it. The third one looked more like a dragon than a snowman.

The kids climbed the crooked steps of the front porch. Jane lifted the heavy knocker and let it fall. They heard it echo inside. Then heavy footsteps came closer and closer. The door slowly creaked open and Boris smiled down at them. Annie couldn't help noticing his pointy eyeteeth were as white as the snow monster's fangs in the front yard.

"It is so nice to have winter visitors," Boris said. "Please come in."

The kids stepped inside the gloomy hallway. Heavy red curtains covered the windows, and they had to blink to get used to the darkness. Once they did they noticed

54

Hilda standing at the top of the curving staircase.

"What's wrong with Kilmer's mother?" Jane whispered.

"She looks like she hasn't slept in a week," Ben told her.

Hilda wasn't dressed in her usual lab coat. Instead, she wore a black robe and fuzzy red slippers. Her hair stuck out even more than normal and dark circles under-lined her eyes. She looked like she had just crawled out of bed.

"Are you okay?" Jane asked. "Do you have the flu?"

Hilda yawned and shook her head. "I am only tired from working all night to make sure Uncle Yetta has a pleasant stay," she explained.

"Well, we brought something that might help," Annie said with her sweetest smile.

Hilda came down the steps and Boris led them all into the living room. Uncle Yetta sat near an open window. The cold winter wind blew the heavy curtains. It was cold inside, so cold Annie could see her breath.

Kilmer sat in a nearby chair. A layer of frost covered his flat haircut, and tiny icicles hung off the spiderwebs on a nearby lamp. Jane glanced out the open window. The three new snow monsters looked like they were peeking inside the window.

"It's too cold in here," Jane whispered. "Maybe we should leave."

"We can't," Annie said softly. "We have to save the Hauntlys — and Christmas!"

Annie put the picnic basket down on the table. "We have a treat for everybody," she said. "A cold-weather treat."

Ben and Jane helped Annie unpack the basket. It was filled with a thermos of hot chocolate. Uncle Yetta backed away, but the warm steam circled his head. Ben pulled mugs out of his sack and Annie poured hot chocolate into them. Jane found marshmallows in her backpack and plunked them in each mug. Then Annie handed Uncle Yetta a steaming mug.

Water started to drip from his heavy winter coat as soon as he took it, and a puddle formed around his feet. Tiny trickles of sweat ran down his forehead and cheeks.

Annie pretended she didn't notice. "We're so glad you came to visit," she told Uncle Yetta.

Ben nodded. "Bailey City is the best place to live."

"That's because it gets so warm in the summer," Jane added.

Uncle Yetta took a handkerchief from his pocket and wiped at the sweat on his forehead.

"Not just warm," Annie said. "Hot. Really hot. So hot steam comes up off the blacktop."

"But it isn't just warm in the summer," Ben said in a polite voice. "Even our winters can be warm."

"Especially when the sun comes out," Jane said. Just then, the sun peeked through a cloud and shone right in on Uncle Yetta's face.

The sun streamed in the window and stretched across the bloodred carpet in the Hauntlys' living room. Uncle Yetta jumped up from the chair. The warm sunbeam made him cringe. A big puddle of water formed around his feet.

"Quick," Kilmer said. "Close the curtains."

Hilda pulled the curtains closed. The room was suddenly thrown into deep shadows. "Do not worry," Hilda said to Uncle Yetta. "I will make sure everything is all right for the rest of your visit."

"Will the sun melt all the snow," Uncle Yetta asked, "and turn this winter wonderland into a steam bath?"

"Not if I can stop it," Hilda told him. "But I must have time."

"I don't think Uncle Yetta has much time," Boris said. "You must hurry, before it's too late!"

11

Monster-cicles

Without another word, Hilda left her guests and rushed from the room, disappearing upstairs.

Kilmer grabbed the mug from his uncle's hand and set it on the table. "Perhaps you would like a frozen pickled pig snout," Kilmer suggested.

"I will fix you one right now," Boris said.

"And I will adjust the thermostat," Kilmer offered and rushed from the room. Soon the temperature dropped even more. Ben's nose turned red and Annie had to put on her gloves.

"If I didn't know better," Jane whispered, "I'd think the Hauntlys were turning us into kid-cicles for Uncle Yetta's afternoon snack!"

Annie's eyes got big. "We'd better get out of here before you give Uncle Yetta any ideas!"

Ben, Jane, and Annie quickly said good-bye to Kilmer's uncle, then they quietly slipped out the front door. They stood on the Hauntly Manor Inn's porch.

"Now we know the truth about Uncle Yetta," Annie said. "I just proved he is the Abominable Snowman."

"No, you didn't," Ben argued. "All we know is that he doesn't like anything hot."

"But if he is the Abominable Snowman," Jane said, "maybe Annie's plan worked. Uncle Yetta will be too worried about melting in the hot Bailey City sun. I bet he leaves for the North Pole and everything will be back to normal."

"Don't be so sure," Ben said. "Look."

The three kids glanced at the sky just as a dark gray cloud moved in front of the sun. Soon giant snowflakes floated down from the sky.

"We've failed," Annie whimpered. "Hilda is already making more snow."

Jane nodded. "Bailey City is doomed to eternal winter!"

"I don't care if Uncle Yetta is the Abominable Snowman," Ben said. "After all, he's Kilmer's uncle."

"Uncle Yetta is nice," Annie admitted. Then she pointed at the three new snow monsters in the front yard. "But I'm not so sure about his snow monster friends."

"I think I know one thing for sure," Ben said as he eyed the snow sculptures. "Those snow monsters aren't delivering my Christmas presents."

"You should stop thinking about yourself," Annie told her brother.

Jane nodded. "The Hauntlys are in danger. Sooner or later the mayor is going to find out about Hilda's snowmaking machine."

"If we all don't turn into monster-cicles first!" Annie said.

12

Christmas Surprise

"Christmas is ruined," Ben moaned and fell down on the couch. "There are no trees, no presents, no cookies, and no candy."

"I haven't had a chance to do my Christmas shopping," Annie said sadly. "I was going to get something extra-special for the Hauntlys."

"Me too," Jane said. "I wanted their first Christmas in Bailey City to be nice."

"What about *my* present?" Ben asked. "What were you going to get *me*?"

"I was thinking about a rock and some sticks," Annie said with a grin. "But the snow is so deep I won't even be able to dig up those!"

Ben, Annie, and Jane were warming up

at Jane's house. Their noses were still a little cold.

"At least we can get warm," Jane said.

Annie nodded. "Think about the poor Hauntlys. They're freezing in their house."

"Their first Christmas in Bailey City won't be a very pleasant one," Jane added. "I wish there was some way we could make it special."

"Wait," Annie said. "I have another idea."

"Forget it," Ben said. "Your last idea almost got us turned into kid-cicles for the Abominable Snowman's snack."

"But you'll like this idea," Annie said. "It'll be fun!"

Jane jumped up as soon as Annie told them her idea. Even Ben sat up on the couch and looked interested.

"You're right," Jane said. "It's the least we can do for the Hauntlys."

Jane hurried to gather everything they needed, then the three kids started cutting and painting and pasting. They made paper chains, bookmarks, and cards. Jane

showed them all how to make tiny folded-paper animals. Soon the table was filled with homemade gifts.

Annie looked up from a newspaper she was cutting. "Now this would be the perfect holiday spot for the Abominable Snowman!" she said, showing Ben and Jane the ad from the newspaper. It pictured a ski resort in Colorado. "The ad says they have snow, snow, and more snow for lots of winter fun."

"Are you thinking what I'm thinking?" Jane asked.

"Let's show it to the Hauntlys," Ben suggested.

They grabbed their coats and gifts and hurried out the door. They didn't stop until they were in front of Hauntly Manor Inn. "I hope this works," Jane whispered when she saw five new snow monsters standing in front of Hauntly Manor Inn. "If it doesn't, the Abominable Snowman and his snow monster pals will be our neighbors."

Annie nodded. "We have to hurry," she said and led Ben and Jane up the sidewalk. Ben pounded on the door and it slowly swung open. Boris stood before them. His skin was an unusual shade of blue, and frost covered the bloodred button of the cape he always wore.

"How nice to see you," Boris said, shivering.

Kilmer hurried to the door. He held his three pet spiders wrapped in a black towel, trying to keep them from freezing.

Hilda peeped over the railing and yelled hello. She was still wearing her bathrobe and slippers, but this time a thick wool cap covered her otherwise unruly hair.

"We wanted to show you something," Annie said. She stepped into Hauntly Manor Inn. It was so cold she wrapped her scarf around her face so that only her eyes and nose were showing. Hilda, Boris, and Kilmer crowded around her as she held up the newspaper ad.

Just then, the floor started to shake. Uncle Yetta stomped into the hallway. "What is going on?" he said.

Ben ducked behind Annie. Jane hid behind the huge wooden door. Annie swallowed and faced Uncle Yetta.

"You mentioned you were very tired from working so hard, Hilda," Annie said and her voice only shook a little. "We found the perfect place for a winter vacation." Then she held out the newspaper ad.

Uncle Yetta leaned over so he could see. Then he slowly began to smile.

13

Snow Vacation

"They're gone!" Jane told Ben and Annie the next morning. She came into the kitchen while they were still eating breakfast.

"What are you talking about?" Ben asked while stuffing his mouth with cereal.

Jane pointed out the window to a huge white van rolling away from the Hauntlys'. "I saw Kilmer on the way over here. He said Uncle Yetta was taking the whole family on a snow vacation to Colorado."

"Wow!" Ben said. "We thought Uncle Yetta was made of snow and all the time he was made of money."

Annie went over to the window. "I still think Uncle Yetta is made out of snow. Come look."

Ben stuffed another spoonful of cereal

into his mouth and went over to the window with Jane and Annie. "What?" Ben asked.

"Don't you see anything unusual?" Annie asked.

"Just the Hauntlys' backyard," Ben said.

Annie nodded. "Their empty backyard."

Jane's eyes got wide. "The snow sculptures are gone," she said.

"They must have taken them with them," Annie agreed. "I bet that was a refrigerated van we saw."

Ben rolled his eyes. "You guys are so nutty I'm surprised a squirrel doesn't try to eat you. There's the answer to your snow monster mystery," he said, pointing at the sky.

Annie squinted out the window. "All I see is the sun," she said finally.

Ben opened the back door. "Exactly. The sun is melting the snow. It doesn't take a genius to figure out that the snow creatures melted away."

"That's good, because you are definitely not a genius," Jane teased.

Annie stooped down and picked up the morning paper off the porch. She smiled when she read the headlines. "Oh, my gosh," she said, "there's been an enormous blizzard in Colorado."

"I hope the Hauntlys will be okay," Jane said.

"Are you kidding?" Annie asked. "Uncle Yetta took the snow with him."

"Do you really think so?" Jane asked.

Annie shrugged. "As long as the Hauntlys live next door, I'll believe anything!"

About the Authors

Marcia Thornton Jones and Debbie Dadey like to write about monsters. Their first series with Scholastic, **The Adventures of the Bailey School Kids,** has many characters who are *monsterously* funny. Now with the Hauntly family, Marcia and Debbie are in monster heaven!

Marcia and Debbie both used to live in Lexington, Kentucky. They were teachers at the same elementary school. When Debbie moved to Aurora, Illinois, she and Marcia had to change how they worked together. These authors now create monster books long-distance. They play hot potato with their stories, passing them back and forth by computer.

About the Illustrator

John Steven Gurney is the illustrator of both **The Bailey City Monsters** and **The Adventures of the Bailey School Kids.** He uses real people in his own neighborhood as models when he draws the characters in Bailey City. John has illustrated many books for young readers. He lives in Vermont with his wife and two children.